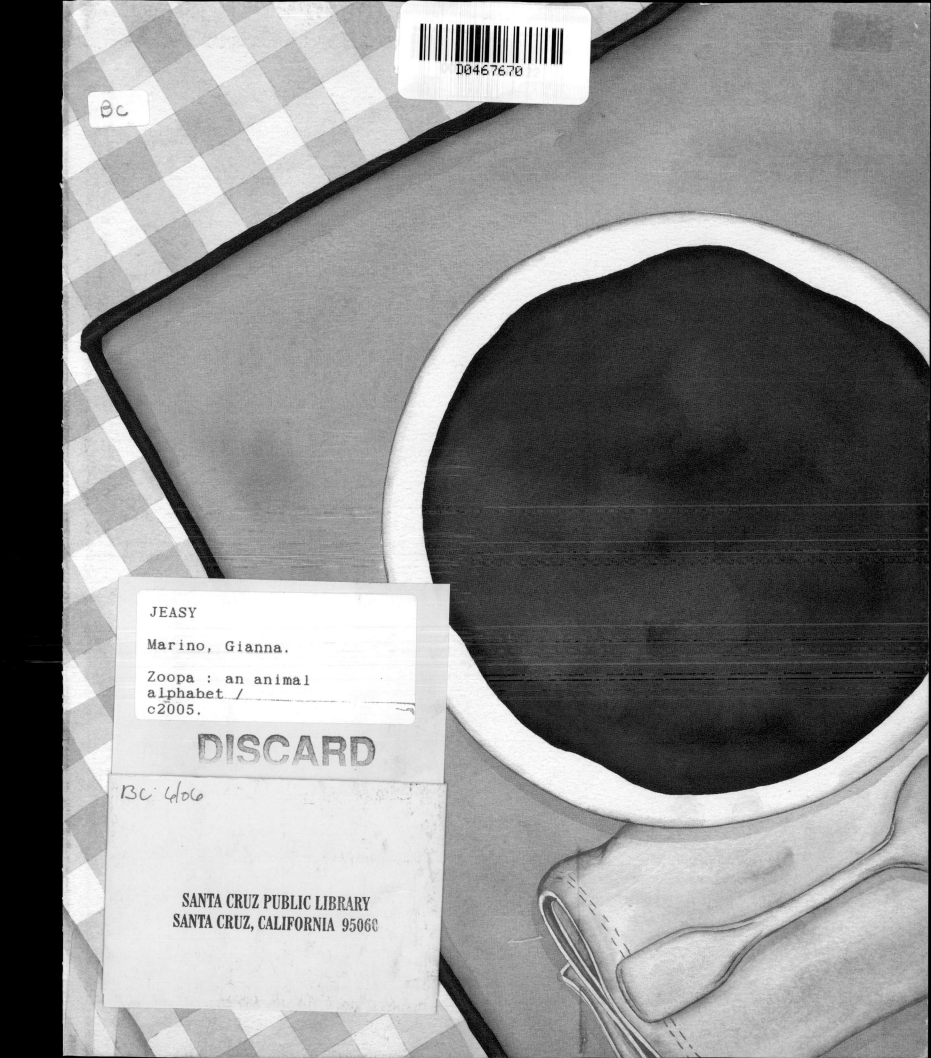

In memory of my father, John,
who could make anyone laugh.
To my mother, Anne,
who encouraged me to be an artist.
And to my family,
Mark, Saskia, and Nicholas.

Book design by Tracy Sunrize Johnson.
Typeset in Bryant.
The illustrations in this book were rendered in gouache.
Manufactured in China.

Library of Congress Cataloging-in-Publication Data
Marino, Gianna.
  Zoopa : an animal alphabet / by Gianna Marino.
     p. cm.
  ISBN 0-8118-4789-6
  1. English language—Alphabet—Juvenile literature.
  2. Animals—Juvenile literature. I. Title.
  PE1155.M364 2005
  428.1'3—dc22   2004063449

Distributed in Canada by Raincoast Books
9050 Shaughnessy Street, Vancouver, British Columbia V6P 6E5

10 9 8 7 6 5 4 3 2 1

Chronicle Books LLC
85 Second Street, San Francisco, California 94105

www.chroniclekids.com

ZOOPA

AN ANIMAL ALPHABET

BY GIANNA MARINO

chronicle books · san francisco

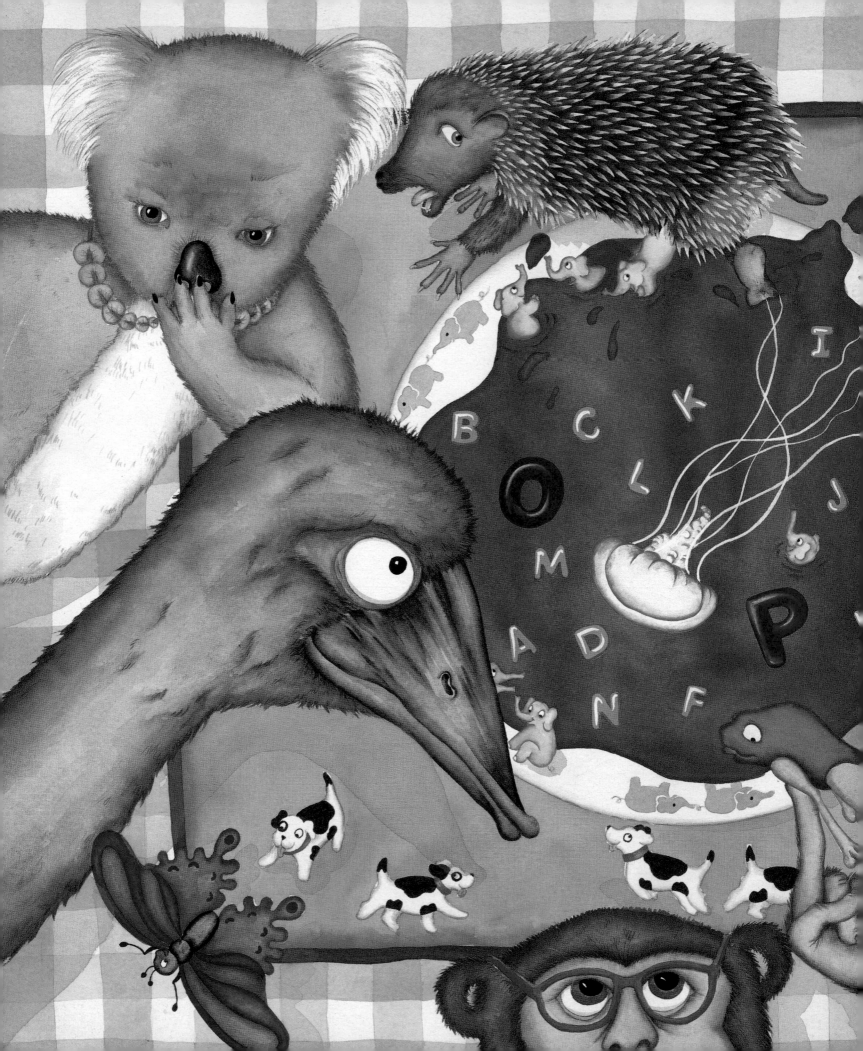

Elephant

Iguana

Grasshopper

Chipmunk

Butterfly

Ant

Dog

Frog

Hedgehog

Nanny Goat

Ladybug

Koala

Jellyfish

Monkey

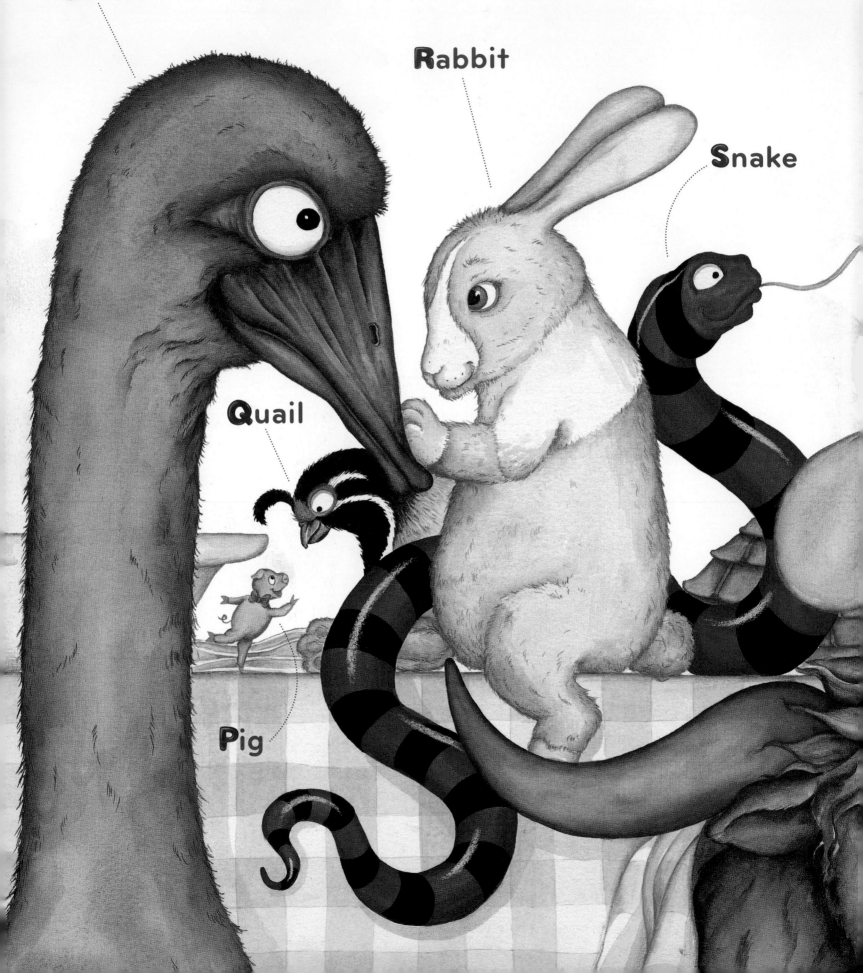

Ostrich

Rabbit

Snake

Quail

Pig

Unicorn

Xenops

Vulture

Zebra

Worm

Turtle

Yak